Sir Pronghorn Academy and Other Stories

TONY SCIARRA

ISBN (paperback): 978-1-0675424-0-5
ISBN (ebook): 978-1-0675424-1-2

Contents

The Majestic but Elusive Rhino-Elephant

I met Alex when we were both pursuing our graduate degrees. I was across the hall from him working on my botany thesis on the biochemical mechanisms used by fungi to detect plant hosts at a distance (a mouthful, I know) while Alex was still struggling for an idea—any idea—in the zoology department. I felt a strange sympathy for this man who resembled a spider. He was all legs and arms and about as hairy as anyone I had ever seen. At six foot three, he was about as thin as a fistful of spaghetti.

Alex was an odd man who came from an odd family. He was the only one of two

brothers, to graduate from university. His younger brother had decided at a young age that it made more sense to wander the woods searching for Sasquatch than to pursue a formal degree. He would wind up managing a cannabis dispensary—when he wasn't searching for Sasquatch, of course. Alex also had a much older cousin, whom I'd met twice. He too was a wandering soul. From the age of seventeen, he'd worked in every province and territory in Canada except for Prince Edward Island. He said that while he'd had a wonderful time in the province, he found it impossible to work there because of something he called "warp". Warp? I think it had something to do with potatoes.

Beyond these two, Alex also had an uncle. A large man with a short beard and thick eyebrows, he claimed to have made several million dollars before he was twenty-five. At twenty-five, he decided to give it all away because he couldn't swim. He said that millionaires lived in mansions, and what is a mansion without a swimming pool?

Regardless of swimming pools, Sasquatches, potatoes, and whatever else, my own work was a complete struggle. None of it was made easier by Alex's presence. Whenever I returned to my office, I could hear him pacing and smacking his head; again and again, at every turn, he would smack, smack, smack. At other times he would run and then jump up and down. I thought maybe he had come to believe the ideas he was searching for were above his head, just out of

reach. Higher … a little higher, maybe. The worst of it was when he did everything at once. I tried whenever possible to give him suggestions, but none satisfied Alex.

I think it was a concussion that finally gave him the subject of his thesis: the rhino-elephant. I had gone into the lab for my usual bout with frustration, when he told me of it. It was a strange beast, he said, which had come about through the unfortunate mating of two very frisky animals. He said he'd seen it in a dream. I thought he was out of his mind.

Over the next two weeks, Alex worked diligently on this bizarre concept. He developed it into a proposal that he then presented to his professors. After they stopped laughing, they told him to leave such things in children's books and to fantasy writers. One of his professors then asked Alex if he would allow the university's medical students to examine him.

"These, after all, are institutions of Banting and Best. It is here that hard work and study meet to produce learning. Alex, this is not a high school, you know," said one of his professors with a broad smile. "We can't tarnish the reputation of this venerable university with this." When Alex protested, they warned him to stop wasting their time. When Alex protested yet more, they told him to leave the building; when he protested still more, they had him forcibly removed.

My heart sank for Alex. I had heard as much of it as possible over the racket being made by the head of zoology, who was desperately trying to get a chicken to lay eggs on command. My situation in the lab was fast deteriorating. The heads of both the zoology and the psychology departments had begun a collaboration. They were both impossible. The zoology prof was a man of fifty who had been divorced twice and was groping his way to a third. The psychology professor, on the other hand, was an attractive blonde woman, who at forty-four, had eyes that screamed no strings and no commitments. Because of their joint collaboration, I was now finding myself in a constant struggle for lab time. And Alex? Well, let's just say there are two types of people: those who come to their senses and those who don't. Alex, of course, belonged firmly in the second camp.

Alex had become more certain than ever he was onto something, but no one would supply Alex with any grant money for such a project. He, instead, resorted to his own meagre savings plus any money he could earn tutoring. I warned him not to let anyone know of his rhino-elephant idea, and he nodded in agreement. It would surely set off a mad stampede in the great hunt for this remarkable creature, he said.

While I continued my research of dropping test-tubes, tipping over trays, and always avoiding the two heads of department, who were always deep in thought, Alex worked hard. Whenever he had enough money saved, he would go off on his mad quest to I-don't-know-where, always on the hunt to prove he wasn't the crackpot he so obviously was. Invariably, each foray ended the same: a forlorn creature, barely human and more spider-like would return, weighed down by yet more grief. At such times, we would head off to a bar next to our university, where I would try my best to explain to Alex the obvious absurdity in breeding such a monstrosity. He rarely listened to me, for he was in a trance, staring deep into the distance, trying to make out where exactly this majestic animal might be.

And then, of course, it happened. One day, and we all know everything happens one day, Alex came into the lab where I was working, with a rush of excitement. He claimed to know where exactly this most elusive of animals made its home. Now, while I won't say where exactly this place might be other than it's not easy to get to, Alex did request that I, his closest of friends (I don't think he had any other friends), come with him to witness the rhino-elephant in all its glory: an animal of myth and legend, yet as real as he was real. I have no idea what myth or what legend he spoke of, but then… Now, normally, I would have declined, but with the constant squabbling from the two heads of the department over who was stealing all the eggs, I was finding it impossible to do any work. When I agreed, Alex became ecstatic.

We packed our bags on a Friday, with all the things you

need for a ludicrous excursion, and we were off the following morning. It took us the better part of that day—navigating several airports in several different countries, losing our bags and then finding them again, only to lose them and find them again. When it seemed we would lose our sanity, we arrived. I didn't know at the time whether it was a good thing or a bad thing, but our hotel sat practically on the edge of the airfield. From our two rooms, which were across from each other, one could not only see the planes lifting off and landing every hour or so, but one could also feel them. Alex was, of course, oblivious to all of this because all he heard were the thundering hooves of rhino-elephants and not those planes. I, on the other hand, could swear that those planes kept getting closer and closer.

As I was about to lie down on my bed, Alex summoned me to his room. He had laid out a large map with X's and O's. A paper map? Yes! He explained that the X's were places of importance. I imagined that was probably where the rhino-elephant was lying in wait for us. The O's, on the other hand, were places where we could find supplies. I was about to mention to Alex that it was interesting how there were vastly more X's than O's, but he had already folded the map back up. Alex then let me know he had booked a guide when we were still in Toronto. He knew the land, and would be waiting for us early the next morning. When I asked where we could find something to eat he looked at me in bewilderment. We had eaten on the plane, he said. That night, between the grumbling of my stomach and the sound of planes lifting off and landing, I barely managed any sleep at all.

When morning came, it came early and honking a horn. Alex was already dressed, screaming for me to get up or he would leave without me. I couldn't decide between the two, except that one of them did come with less screaming. I got up and got dressed. Big mistake. And the man outside? Well, he did know how to honk a horn. Leaving the hotel I saw our guide for the first time. He was a young man in military fatigues, and he sat in a jeep that must have been older than him. While we tossed our supplies into the back, he drummed on the steering wheel to music I thought was about as imaginary as the rhino-elephant. And then off we thundered—literally.

It would take us less than half an hour before civilization vanished. Our guide, it appeared to me, knew less of this place than we did. The only thing he seemed to know well was how to go very fast and then very slow. Whenever I asked how much longer it would be, he would simply nod and smile.

Finally! Finally! After what felt like an eternity (yes, an eternity has a feeling), we arrived at the edge of jungle that looked no different than the one we had spotted an hour before. It appeared, though, that Alex was of a different mind. He was very pleased with this particular shade of colour. Pulling our supplies from the jeep, our guide let us know in no uncertain terms that he would only make the return trip in several days if we paid him twice what we had paid to get there. He then said something about my sister that I didn't quite understand since I don't have a sister, but still, we agreed. Just before he left us, he told us to watch out for the old fool by the tree.

I was surprised there could be anyone to watch out for, but yet there he was, under a tree that had seen many, many better days. There really is no place on this earth where humans don't walk. As our guide sped away, I wondered what I had gotten myself into. While I study botany, it is one thing to study plants, but quite another to get lost in the study of plants. As I contemplated my demise, Alex walked over to the grizzled man who rested against that grizzled tree. Just above his head was a knothole the size of a fist. Before I died in that jungle, I promised myself I would squeeze Alex's head inside it.

English, it turns out, is a very popular language, and this man spoke a version of it himself. He leaned against the tree, and I kid you not, waved a two-meter-long staff back and forth, which he said was necessary to keep the air in motion or else it would turn to stone. When Alex asked, very slowly, if he had seen any strange animal roaming this jungle, he answered that he had seen such an animal many, many times. Giving us some roots and herbs, he told us that they come whenever you are ready. I had no idea what that meant. Alex, as you can well imagine, was over the moon, and that, curiously enough, would be where we would soon end up.

While I wanted to rest, Alex was adamant that we start immediately. I pleaded my case, but it's impossible to reason with someone who has destiny on his mind. He made clear we didn't have time to waste, and so I feebly relented and we set off. We ventured first in one direction, then in another; we circled in this direction, then in the other. We, in fact, went so far that we found nowhere again and again. It was only because we stopped frequently to mark our position that we didn't get completely lost. It soon became clear, even to Alex, that it was best to bed down for the night and rest in anticipation of that most incredible event.

That night, Alex insisted we should take some of the roots and herbs, for they would surely help us find the animal. They didn't taste bad, but what visions! Through that terrible night, I remember very vividly being chased by a serpent and clawed by what appeared to be a terrifying spider. I felt I would never escape. It went on and on. I didn't know what horrors Alex endured, but come morning, he was in excellent spirits, ready for the challenge ahead.

I didn't have time to string two words together before we set off once more. We travelled so endlessly that we finally ended up at our original location. The grizzled tree with the knot hole was right in front of us. The only thing missing was the old man, who had probably gone off in search of more herbs. Before I was able to point this out to Alex, I realized he had spotted something. I retreated to a safe distance, but Alex, ever the brave soul, had no intention of missing his destiny. He had been waiting far too long for the rhino-elephant of legend to let it escape into the jungle. I was so tired and woozy that all I could do was watch as Alex tried to draw the beast towards him. With arms and legs flailing, he hurled himself into the clearing.

Now, here is the thing: while they don't teach it in schools, I still to this day firmly believe every child from the age of seven should be instructed to never, ever get in the way of a rhinoceros. This animal, furious, Furious! that a spider dared stand in its way, caught Alex from the side and, without piercing him, lifted that spider, and with a sweep of its powerful neck, sent him flying into the tree. The creature, having poor vision, spotted the knothole and plunged its horn into it. The force was so great that it passed through to the other side. As I looked on in disbelief, for one split second, whether through the wooziness of the night before or just exhaustion, I imagined the rhino-elephant in all its savage glory. Unfortunately, it lasted just that split second, because the animal pulled its horn from the tree and trotted back from whence it came.

And is the rhino-elephant actually real? Well, I have to admit, finding such a creature is about as likely as finding an old man in the jungle with roots and herbs, or a solitary rhino roaming without armed protection guarding it against poachers. And Alex? Well, he isn't dead, if that's what you're wondering. What I've been told is that he and his brother hunt Sasquatch whenever they have enough money saved up.

Elephants

I live in a secluded area on the eastern fringe of Toronto called the Rouge. Here, I share my life with all manner of creatures, very few of which are human. Of those that are, one is a neighbour who is wont to keep her outdoor security lights on throughout the night until morning to ward off prowlers. With the lights acting as a beacon, my house is regularly invaded by deer mice from late fall until deep into the winter. It was this that put me in mind of an experience related to me by a close friend, who has since sadly passed away.

There was a man of medium build—he was not too short and not too tall, neither thin nor fat—who lived on the twenty-fifth floor of a condominium building in the heart of a major city I can't recall the name of. Surrounded by a vista of cement, glass, and steel, he lived a carefree existence, oblivious to all the challenges that lurked down below. One day, a day no different than the day before nor the one that would follow, a salesman knocked on his door.

"Hello, sir. May I ask, have you been having problems with elephants?" the man began.

"Elephants? Why, I … I don't understand?" he replied.

"You know, elephants, elephants. Six tons of heft, with noses—well, a lip really—down to the ground. You know, elephants."

"No, I haven't had any problems with elephants."

"Well, you see, many of the residents in this fine building—and it is a very fine building, I might add—have had some very difficult experiences with these ponderous beasts. Now, as you must surely understand, no one—and I mean no one—wishes a run-in with such animals. So … " he said, and he drew himself back as if reaching for a net to trap the terrible animal or maybe it was meant for something much, much smaller. "I'm here to offer you protection against these most difficult of creatures. You see, I have here a bell, a most magical bell, that if rung for a full fifteen minutes—not ten, not twenty, but a full fifteen minutes every night at eleven—will completely protect you from elephants. Now, this bell usually retails for $500, but on this most propitious of days, it is being offered for only $250."

"But I've never heard of elephants making their way up elevators before," the astute condo-dweller asserted.

"That, sir, is the very reason for its necessity. I have, and I say this to you in the strictest of confidence," said the salesman, bending closer, "spoken to several of your neighbours on the lower floors. They have been witnessing them entering, not only the lobby, but they have even been witnessing them wedging their huge girths into the elevators. You have had the misfortune, I imagine, of malfunctioning elevators? That, sir, is the end result of this most unwelcome parade."

The man was confused. And of course, concerned.

"It would be unfortunate," the salesman continued, " if one day they decided to climb the outside of this very fine building to make their way through that open window," and he pointed to the closed window in the apartment.

"Climbing the outside of a building?" the man scoffed. "Preposterous! How could they do such a thing?"

"With ropes and grappling hooks, sir. You are surrounded by many, many envious people. They have been supplying these awful beasts with all manner of tools. And, I might add, how to use them. They are very intelligent creatures, these elephants. Very quick to learn, you know."

"But wouldn't a broom … you know, shoo them away?"

"A broom! Why, sir, these are monstrous creatures. They might use it against you," the salesman laughed.

The condo dweller's concern was now replaced by palpable fear. He could almost hear the violent trumpeting and stamping of their feet over his beautiful shag carpeting.

"So, sir, should I leave you to this terrible event or will you, like all your neighbours, choose to ward off these awful creatures with this bell?"

The man stood, and he stared. He then turned to look into his beautiful apartment. It was so smartly decorated, so carefully arranged, but all for naught. The animals would surely tip over all the cabinets, make a mockery of his crystal chandelier, and they would very definitely destroy his newly purchased Victorian console table. What a calamity, what a calamity, and all because of jealous people and some ungrateful, vengeful animals. Why, why, why? Why were they so unwilling to stay put in the jungle where they belonged? It just wasn't right. It just wasn't. He knew he needed to have that bell, and very quickly he did. From then on, every night at eleven he could be heard ringing the bell for a full fifteen minutes. Now, while he was definitely protected from rampaging elephants, he had, unfortunately, become a complete nuisance to his neighbours.

My Son David

My son David is a very imaginative little boy. At eight years of age, he sees so much wonder in the world that it fills me with joy. It is a privilege to be able to see the world through his eyes. When my son asked me a most peculiar question, I should have spent more time with David than I did, but it was his bedtime and I was too tired.

"Daddy, what happens if the monsters don't come back?" he asked.

I at first mistook what he had said and answered, "Don't worry, David, they can never hurt you. They never come to this house."

"No, no, Daddy. What happens if they don't come back?"

"Come back?"

"Yes, Daddy. What happens if they don't come back?. They always come back, but what happens if they stay away?"

"I guess ... they just disappear."

"But I don't want them to disappear."

"Davey, what are you saying? Where are these monsters?"

"Why, they're everywhere, Daddy."

"Are they here now? In this room?"

"No, not now."

"Are they in this house?"

"Sometimes."

"When?"

"Sometimes."

"Do they scare you?"

"No, no daddy they don't. They're nice monsters."

I was lost and didn't know what more to say. "If you see them, could you tell me or Mommy?"

"Okay."

"I'll leave the lights on in the hall, okay?"

"Sure, Daddy." And I made my way out of his room and down the stairs.

Sienna, my wife, was curled up on the couch watching an episode of a crime drama we had taped the night before. Tall and thin, she was like a cat. She cut her hair short to look more professional, but she was all heart. Her good nature actually helped her business as a mortgage consultant because people knew she cared, and that was how I met her. I had been thinking of buying a condo at the time, and she was recommended to me by my realtor. While I never bought the condo, I did marry Sienna, and we ended up buying a house instead. We were in our late twenties at that point; we had David when we were both twenty-nine. When we tried to have a second child, hoping for a girl, it turned out not to be, and that was fine for us.

"So what were you two talking about up there?" and she leaned against me as I sat down beside her.

"Davey asked what would happen if the monsters don't come back."

"What?" she said, drawing back.

"Yeah, he asked me what would happen if the monsters don't come back."

"Not that again," she said, and looked down. She then turned off the television and sat there pensively.

"What? What's the matter?" I laughed.

"I don't get it." She shook her head.

"What?" I asked again with another laugh.

"I don't know. It's just that David asked me that last week."

"He did?"

"Yeah, I was closing the window in his bedroom after putting him to bed, and he screamed to leave it open. I jumped—I mean, he scared me—and that's when he said that the monsters always use the window, and I needed to leave it open or they couldn't get back."

"So what did you do?"

"Well, I told him that this time they would need to stay outside. I mean, it was cold. It's still May, after all."

"Davey does have an imagination."

"Yes, he does … " she trailed off.

"Do you think he's seeing things?"

"David? No. Absolutely not."

"Did he say anything after that?" I asked.

"No, he didn't. I mean, I was busy the next day with work and all. Let me think, let me think. This would be last week. Let me think, let me think …"

"It was probably nothing," I reassured her, and turned the television back on.

It was a few days later that I received a frantic phone call at the engineering firm I work for. It was from Sienna, telling me that she was at Sick Kids Hospital with David. He had fallen down the stairs at home and broken his arm. I was shocked. I told my supervisor I needed to go because of a family emergency and raced to the hospital as quickly as I could. It was in the emergency department that I found them. I could see that David's arm was in a cast. He was mildly sedated, and Sienna was upset. I held her and asked her what had happened.

"The monsters! The monsters! David said they told him to fall down the stairs."

"What are you saying?"

"I was working in my office downstairs when I heard him fall. I ran and picked him up, and while I was rushing him here, I asked him what had happened. That's when he told me the monsters, the monsters."

David was too sedated to speak, but I knew we needed to talk to him to understand what was going on.

"Have you talked to anyone here at the hospital?"

"Yes, yes. I talked to a pediatrician. While they were putting the cast on his arm, she came in and asked what had happened."

"You told her about the monsters?"

"Yes, yes, I did. She told me there was nothing to worry about. That it was likely a phase and that as long as he was still young and doing well at home and at school, it would go away on its own."

"And that was all?" I asked.

"She recommended a child psychologist here in the hospital."

"What did you say?"

"Anthony, I just don't know what he means by it."

"You did say yes?"

"Of course I did. I just don't get it."

I stroked Sienna's hair and assured her it was nothing and not to worry. We would find out everything was fine at David's appointment, which had been set for Monday, just six days away. David would stay in the hospital that evening, so when visiting hours were over, we said goodbye to David. He was so groggy, I wondered if he even heard us tell him how much we loved him. The drive home was like the rest of the evening: we barely said anything.

On the Sunday before our appointment, Sienna and I were alone sitting on the couch, deep in our thoughts, when I heard a loud crash from David's room. We both raced up the stairs, Sienna stumbling, me practically falling over her. When we got to David's room, we found him on his bed. The small bookcase next to it, where he kept his books and favorite toys, was tipped over. David looked frightened.

"Mommy, the monsters! The monsters need to come in through the window. Please, Mommy, keep the window open, or they won't be able to come back. They need to come back, or they can't go home."

"Please!" Sienna screamed, clutching him. "Don't say that, don't say that!"

I looked at the window and could see that it was only half open. Outside, I could hear the last of the day welcoming the night.

The next day, I accompanied Sienna and David to the child psychologist. The man's office was not very large; it had a desk and some comfortable chairs, and in the corner were stacked a variety of toys. He welcomed us in, and we all sat down. He was a pleasant older man with greying hair, who spoke slowly and occasionally repeated himself. We were asked the basics about our son: his age, his life before the experiences we were there for, his situation at school, and his friends. Sienna explained that everything had been fine until recently when he had begun talking about monsters.

David sat quietly; his arm in a cast, he seemed confused by what was going on around him. It was at this point the child psychologist asked us to leave so he could talk to David alone. He told us we could go down to the cafeteria and get ourselves a coffee because it would take at least thirty-five minutes. We looked up at the clock in his office. It was 1:10. Sienna kissed David and told him we would be back soon, that everything was alright, and he should tell the man everything he knew. David nodded and watched us leave.

In the cafeteria, we sat and waited. We must have been there for at least seven minutes before we realized we had not ordered any coffee. I went over and brought back two. Sienna broke into tears. As she sat quietly sobbing, I put my arm around her shoulder. We decided it would probably be better to sit in the waiting room, so we left our coffees untouched and went back up. It was now just past 1:30. The waiting room was empty except for ourselves and a small boy, David's age, who clutched his mother. The little boy was scared, and his mother tried to calm him with a story about a wonderful place where candies grew in gardens and people spoke a cloud language.

I listened until the receptionist's voice brought me back, calling Sienna's name. We got up and went back inside the office. While David was still sitting in his chair as before, he was now sucking on a lollipop. The receptionist, who had followed us in, was told to take David outside. Sienna held him and told David to go with the nice lady. David nodded and left the room. We waited while the doctor sat scribbling notes in his journal.

"Now, Sienna and Anthony, I've spoken to David, and he tells me there's nothing wrong."

"What about the monsters?" Sienna blurted.

"Well, the monsters," he said, drawing himself back into his chair. "Many children have, at your son's age, such a fantastical imagination. You see, right now I can't say anything. These things generally pass on their own. As long as there are no other negative changes—in his mood, his sleep, his interactions with other children—it would be best to let him work through this on his own."

"But what did he say about the monsters?" Sienna demanded. "Why does he keep talking about monsters needing to come back to his room?"

"What he said," he replied with a kind smile, "was that they need to come back so they can go home. He doesn't fear them. He just wants them to go home."

"Home? I don't understand," I asked.

"Well, David believes they need to go home. I wouldn't worry. Just let him work through it."

"Well, what are we supposed to do? Leave his window open at night?" Sienna said in exasperation.

"If that's what it takes, leave it open." Then he added, "For now. Over time, he should forget all about this, but for now, leave it open."

"And he'll just forget it all?" Sienna asked.

"Yes, he should." Then he added, " You needn't worry as long as he does well at school, sleeps well, eats well, and keeps up with his friends." He then smiled, and repeated, "There's really nothing to worry about."

He ushered us out of his office. We didn't know what to think. In the waiting room, David had finished his lollipop and was sitting quietly in a corner chair. The little boy, I could see, was still clutching his mother in fear while she rocked him back and forth. She had begun to cry.

"Come on, David, we're going home now," and Sienna reached out her hand.

David took Sienna's hand and said, "It's okay, mommy."

Sienna was about to cry when she heard him say that, but I squeezed her shoulder, and we walked out to the car.

On the ride home, Sienna sat in silence, so I asked, "So, David, that was a big day we had, huh?"

He nodded his head.

"Everything's okay?"

And he nodded again.

"You know you can tell us anything, right, David?"

And he nodded yet again. He then said, "Daddy, please, please leave the window open," to which Sienna squeezed the car seat.

"Sure, David. Sure. We can do that, but you know it doesn't always have to be like that, right?"

David didn't say anything and instead looked out the window.

When we got home, we spent the rest of the day with David playing Monopoly. It seemed like old times. David was such a wonderful little boy. Whenever he won, he would shriek with his beautiful little laugh. We ordered pizza and talked about his classes and the baseball game we would be going to the following week. Then it was time to get ready for bed. I wrestled him up the stairs, and like so many times before, I had to force him to brush his teeth. When he complained that he couldn't because of the cast, I reminded him he was right-handed, which made him laugh. Finally, David slipped into bed, but as I was about to turn and leave, he demanded, "Daddy, the window needs to be open."

I walked to the window and opened it. The night air was not as cool as it had been just a few short weeks before. I could hear the slight rustling of the leaves that I had left to collect in the flower beds the previous fall. It would soon be summer, and time to cut the grass all over again. As I looked out into the twilight, I could make out the strangest of shapes; at times they appeared to tumble like a ball only to rise up and run. Sometimes they seemed to leap into the air as if they were trying to grab something. I couldn't make out much else except that they were definitely making their way towards the house.

The Views Are Wonderful

When Alex and Susan married, they married with a plan. In Year One they would have a daughter, in Year Three they would add a son, and by their seventh year they would be living in their own house in the best neighbourhood in the city. It didn't turn out quite that way. Although they did have two children by Year Three, they were both girls, and as for that house in the best neighbourhood? Well, that would have to wait and wait and wait. By their twelfth year of marriage, it was clear they had to do something. Out went the house, out went the best neighbourhood, and in came anything else.

Alex and Susan called in a real estate agent and made clear they wanted a three-bedroom condominium with a view. The man looked at their budget, smiled and took them on a whirlwind tour of the "city's views". In the three months of that contract, they saw views of railroad tracks, cemeteries, incinerators, and factories.

When their contract came to a close, they knew they had to make a change, so they called up a new real estate agent and made it clear to her they wanted a beautiful view. She looked at their budget, smiled and took them down to a condo on the waterfront. Just beyond a stretch of open land was a magnificent view of Lake Ontario. When the realtor made clear that she too was planning on buying, they knew it was perfect. Pricey, but perfect. With fingers crossed, they put in an offer, and surprisingly, it was accepted. They were now the proud owners of a seventh-floor, three-bedroom condominium that looked directly onto Lake Ontario.

During the next three months, Alex and Susan sorted and marked all their possessions. They then, with the help of several close friends, piled all their furniture and precious items into a rental truck, and off to their new home they went. Years One and Two, the view was magnificent, but then in Year Three everything changed. In that year, Alex and Susan started seeing hoarding going up around what they had assumed was a park. A low-slung office building was quickly constructed next to it, and units in a new condominium building became available.

Being underwater is a terrible thing, whether in the lake or on dry land seven stories up. Unable to sell, they watched a beautiful twenty-eight-story building with glass so shiny it was blinding go up. Normally that would have been a problem, but luckily for Alex and Susan, the building was so close, and ever so tall, that what they mostly saw was darkness.

With the view of Lake Ontario gone, the one consolation they could still draw upon was that their real estate agent had not been lying. On a Sunday, while Alex and

Susan were sitting on their balcony enjoying a cup of coffee, they saw her down below. Newly married, the woman and their original real estate agent were busily unloading boxes, for they were now the proud owners of a condominium with a magnificent view of the lake.

The Hand that Claps Last Claps Loudest

When I was many years younger than I am now, I attended a chemistry course at my university with the goal of becoming something I had no business being. In my first tutorial of my only year in the program, I entered a classroom that, while small, was made large by how few people there were. In the back of this virtually empty room, I passed a man who was sitting with a very beautiful woman. They seemed completely devoid of anything to say. They both sat, and they sat, and all they did was sit. Several seats nearer the front, I spied another woman who was sitting all by herself. I, all alone and with nothing to do, sat beside her and started a conversation. I talked about one fantastical thing and then another impossible event, and she laughed. We sat like this until class began, and when it ended, she went her way, and I went mine.

At my next tutorial, I was left surprised. The man, who I mentioned earlier, had left his beautiful girlfriend to now sit in my old seat. Now, one hand clapping makes for little sound, and so there they sat, and sat and sat. With nothing to do, and not wanting the beautiful woman to be all alone, I sat beside her. And now all these years later, whenever we fuck, we think of opportunities that are presented and taken away, only to be greeted with possibilities never anticipated but fully appreciated.

The Man Who Stepped Outside of Himself

When the Conleys married, they married for better or worse, through thick and thin, and their first years proved to be very happy ones. They travelled to faraway places like Rome, Sao Paulo, and Jakarta. They ate at fine restaurants. They owned a house in Moore Park, a cottage in Muskoka. They lived a very expensive lifestyle. Even though Stephen held a high-paying job as Chief Process Engineer at Select Foods International, and his wife, Isabel, was an insurance broker for Genuine Insurance, their expenses became too much for them. Bills piled up, deadlines went scattering by, and the strain on their marriage grew and grew, turning all the happiness of their early years into distant memories. Arguments and recriminations followed them everywhere. Days now began with a quarrel and ended with yet another one. Weeks, months; the fights never stopped. Not, that is, until the day they were threatened with foreclosure.

Their bank requested an urgent meeting for the following day, or there would be consequences. Until then, they had always been able to get extensions on their mortgage and other debts. This time, though, it was different; the envelope had come by way of courier. It was then that Stephen announced he had stepped outside of himself.

Isabel was at first bewildered, then horrified by the possibility that her husband might be trying to escape the predicament that was as much his fault as hers. And yet Stephen, a medium-sized man with easy features, continued to insist in a very calm tone that he was no longer inside himself and had left for the outside.

Isabel looked around. She began searching for where he might have gone. She looked behind the small couch he was sitting on in their home office; she thumbed through the stacks of magazines on the desk, but wherever she looked, Stephen would insist she would not find him there because he was now above it all. Isabel looked up to the ceiling but could not find him there, so she turned and took a good look at Stephen. Seated on the couch, he looked back at her with such a serene calm that it terrified her.

The only thing Isabel knew was she could not go to their bank alone. She was not going to carry all the responsibility herself. Stephen was definitely not going to get away that easily and yet … Stephen again informed her he was now above it all; he could see himself so clearly and was not a part of it anymore. Isabel knew she had to close the windows and doors, or he might escape completely … but then what?

Over the following hour, Isabel stared at Stephen, who seemed to have become as immobile as a statue. She thought and thought as to what she should do. The bank appointment was for the following day, and since Stephen earned more money than her, he needed to be there if they were going to convince the bank to give them more time.

Now, Isabel was a very methodical woman. She may have been small; she may have seemed frail, but she was also methodical. Once she had exhausted all other avenues, she knew she had to call her brother, Robert. Robert worked as a delivery manager at a well-established courier company. Isabel reached him at work. She let him know what had just happened and that she was at her wits' end as to what to do. Robert told his little sister not to worry and that he would be over in the next hour.

Isabel was confident her brother would be able to make Stephen step back inside himself. Robert was, after all, a burly man who worked out quite regularly at a local gym. As time went on, she became more and more confident she had made the right decision and began to relax. But then again … every time she looked across at Stephen, he looked back with that same serene, calm smile. It unnerved her.

An hour later, Isabel heard a knock at the front door. It was Robert. Isabel took him to the home office and, opening the door, she pointed at Stephen.

"See," she cried. "He's stepped outside of himself."

Robert looked at Stephen. He snapped his fingers. Nothing. He slapped him. Nothing. Robert then pressed his head against Stephen's chest. He definitely heard the thump-thump of a heartbeat. Stephen was still salvageable, he thought. He turned to Isabel and reassured her that everything was under control.

"What did he tell you?"

"He told me he'd stepped outside of himself."

"Anything else?"

"He said he'd stepped outside of himself and that he was looking at himself from above. That's when I closed the window."

Robert looked across at the window, which was in fact closed, and was pleased at Isabel's quick thinking. If Stephen was floating about, it would be necessary to collect him, he thought.

"Do you have a bag? A container of some kind?" he asked.

"Well, there is an ice cream bucket in the recyclables."

"Does it still have the lid?"

"Well, yeah, it's one of those …" and Isabel made a gesture.

"Good, good. Now, get me a vacuum cleaner and the bucket."

Isabel didn't know what Robert was planning to do, but she trusted him, and closing the door behind her, she went off to collect the bucket from the recyclable bin and the vacuum cleaner from the utility closet. When she returned, Robert told Isabel to close the door. Then, pulling the wand from the machine and turning it on, he made numerous passes around the room. He waved the wand back and forth, again and again, for several minutes. He then asked Isabel to bring over the ice cream bucket, which she did. He asked her to remove the lid, which she did. With a very quick motion he dumped everything into it, ensuring nothing escaped. He then snapped on the lid.

"Now we've got him!" Robert shouted with satisfaction.

"But what about Stephen?"

Oh yes, what about Stephen.

"Do you have a sack?"

"A sack?"

"Yeah, a bag. Something big enough for Stephen here," and he thumped Stephen on the forehead.

"Oh, now I understand," and Isabel ran down to the basement where she had stored the bag that had once held their mattress.

When she returned, Robert asked, "Are there any holes?"

"I don't think so," Isabel said.

"Well, check to make sure. We don't want any more of Stephen getting out," he said with a smile.

Isabel examined the bag as closely as she could and noticed the only rips were near its mouth.

"They won't matter," said Robert. "Just get me some tape."

Isabel went back to the utility closet to get some strong electrical tape. When she got back, Robert was already fitting Stephen into the bag.

"Yeah, that'll do," he said. He took the tape, tore off a long strip, and taped the bag as tightly as he could. "He won't be able to get out of there," he laughed. "Tomorrow, you can take him to the bank with you."

"You'll come? I mean, I can't carry him by myself."

This was going to be costly, Robert thought, but he couldn't let his little sister down.

"What time do you have to be at the bank?"

"One o'clock."

It was definitely going to be costly. "I'll be over at twelve, and I'll carry him over."

Isabel was thankful, and after Robert left, she went to bed secure in the knowledge Stephen would be at the bank with her.

At twelve noon the next day, Robert came and carried Stephen over to his truck. While he was fitting Stephen into the cargo box, Isabel got inside the truck with the ice cream bucket. The drive wasn't very long, but it still gave Isabel enough time to work out what she would say to convince the bank manager to give them an extension on their mortgage. It just wasn't right for the bank to take their house.

When they finally arrived at the bank, Robert draped Stephen over his shoulder while Isabel carried the bucket. Making their way inside, everyone went silent. Isabel recognized her case manager, alone in her office, talking on the phone. Isabel motioned Robert towards her, and he carried Stephen into her office. When Robert tried to prop Stephen against the wall, he slipped to the floor. The case manager slowly lowered the phone, then raised it quickly. "I'll call you back," she said.

Robert told Isabel he had to leave. He could still manage a few hours of work. She thanked him for all he had done, and he left.

"Who is this?" her case manager asked in horror. She could clearly make out the contours of a body.

Isabel, embarrassed by all that Stephen had put her through, explained, "It's only Stephen. He stepped outside of himself, so we had to bring him in like this."

Her case manager didn't say a thing.

"See?" and Isabel tore open the bag to expose Stephen's head. He had a most serene smile, but he was very, very dead.

Those Who Live in Glass Houses Don't Throw Stones

Tristan was his name, and he was definitely not an English knight. No, Tristan was a tall, thin man who moved very much like a nervous giraffe; always on the alert for a stalking lion or, what was more likely, creditors. He had trained as a builder, and for the first number of years in that trade, he had operated as a typical one. During that time, he helped create the usual ordinary constructions we see all around us. When boredom set in, however, Tristan decided he wanted to build something unique, so he designed the glass house. Top, bottom, side to side, up, down, and all around: every bit of it glass, whether it be the roof, the beams, the ducts, or the stairs. It was 2500 square feet of oven in the summer and freezer in the winter. The house was to be the perfect addition for the buyer with too much money and not enough sense as to what to do with it.

In total, Tristan sold absolutely none of them. At this point in time, Tristan decided to start The Institute for the Study of Past Lives. No connection? It really doesn't matter. To this very day, almost no one knows that it ever even existed. In the days and months that followed, he placed ads and sent out flyers. Almost no one read them, but of those who did, fourteen showed up. Of those fourteen, only nine remained to witness the final act.

To those who showed up, Tristan spoke of Napoleon; he spoke of Alexander the Great; he spoke of Julius Caesar. In total, he had assembled a fine collection of twenty-three illustrious men and two women. Did it matter that some overlapped? No! In the total of ten sessions that he held on the factory floor of a building soon to be condemned, it would be during the seminal seventh that Tristan would meet his fate.

Out of the group of nine followers that still remained at this point was a woman. While tall and lean like Tristan, she definitely didn't move like a nervous giraffe. No, she moved more like a lioness stalking prey. The woman reminded Tristan of a girl from his college days who had always rebuffed his advances. In the first six sessions, Tristan propositioned her again and again, and as in college, the results proved to be the same. It was in that momentous seventh session that the woman finally made her move.

"Tristan, is it right that these men, and they are mostly men, have escaped justice for their crimes?" she asked. "After all, Tristan, was it not the case that most of what they did was criminal?"

Tristan was shocked. Twenty-three men and two women, and almost every one of them a monster.

"We must prosecute these, these figures for the crimes they have committed, don't you think?"

Tristan was shocked. Twenty-three men and two women, and almost every one of them a monster.

Before Tristan could reclaim the room, it claimed him. And as the mob had done during the French Revolution, so it did once more, sweeping everything before it. In what seemed like the blink of an eye, his Institute for the Study of Past Lives was transformed into the Society Entrusted with the Prosecution of Past Lives. And of course, Tristan became Exhibits A, B, C … since only he had lived such an incredibly rich existence.

Rape, murder, pillage: Tristan had indeed been a very busy boy (and occasionally girl). Times were different then, he insisted. It doesn't matter, they replied. A crime is a crime, and justice must be meted out. But what of all the good deeds? What of all the bad ones? Justice must be meted out. Are history books to be trusted? Yes! Justice must be meted out.

Trials are curious things. They seem to end where they begin, and this one was no different. What could possibly be a just punishment for a historical figure as deplorable as Tristan? What could possibly redeem the many who had suffered so cruelly from Tristan's terrible acts?

It was the beginning of the tenth and final session that things took a most terrible turn. It was then that the eight men and one woman wheeled in the guillotine. Yes, they had built themselves a guillotine—and a very good one at that. While they extended it to its full height, Tristan, ever the nervous giraffe, saw his ultimate creditor and made a desperate dash for the door. Blocked, he made one, two circuits of the factory floor. His head and legs seemed at times to be on opposite sides of the room. It would have been exceedingly difficult to trap such a creature, but unfortunately for Tristan, it turned out to be fairly straightforward when he tried to wedge himself through a barred window. Screams or not, he was dragged over to that device, and his head was neatly fitted into the stock. In an instant, Tristan's past lives and his present one came together inside the glass house of his severed head.

Jeremy's New Car

When Jeremy turned sixteen, he earned his driver's license. Whenever he drove, he drove his father's 4x4, and for that, Jeremy always needed his permission. Jeremy, so wanted a car of his own, but his parents made it clear to him that he would have to show that he had the maturity necessary to own a car. He would need to buy it with his own money. Over the course of the following year, Jeremy worked at a burger place; he worked as a busboy at a pizzeria, and he cut his neighbours' grass.

By the end of that year, he still did not have enough saved to buy the perfect car. While that was an impossibility, maybe it could still buy him enough of a car to take his girlfriend, Shannon, around the city. Jeremy knew of a used car dealership his friends had bought theirs from, so he and his best friend Mike went over to check out what was available. When they got to Tom's Autos it quickly became obvious that everything was far too expensive. There were rows and rows of cars, but not one he could afford. It turned out even a down payment would be a stretch. He didn't know what to do. As he and Mike were about to walk off the car lot, Tom of Tom's Autos approached them.

"So, gentlemen, have you made up your minds?"

"Nah. I don't think I can afford anything here," Jeremy laughed nervously.

"No, don't say that. This is Tom of Tom's Autos. Nobody ever walks away from Tom without a car. Why we have this beauty that just came in. It's $12,999, almost new."

"Too much, too much."

"How about this jewel of a car?" and Tom walked over to a yellow hatchback Jeremy could never see himself driving." I can let you have it for $10,999."

"Nah, but what about this one?" Jeremy had always loved the blue 4x4 his father drove, and while this one was an ugly green, he knew a paint job would be an easy fix.

"Well, that's a beautiful truck, but as you can see from the sticker, it's $11,999. Look, son, tell me how much you can afford, and maybe we can find a car that can fit your budget."

"I've only got, like $3,000," he said sheepishly.

"Not to worry, not to worry. I think I've got something just for you," and he led the two boys to the far end of the lot. When they got there, Tom showed Jeremy and his friend a car that must have been at least twelve years old and carried quite a bit of rust. The thing had 87,000 km on it but still had a sticker price of $5,999.

"That's still too much," Jeremy said with a defeated look in his eyes.

"Son, I never do this, but let me knock it down to, lets say, $5,000, and all you have to do is pay me $1,000 up- front and we'll finance the rest." When he noticed Jeremy was somewhat confused, he added, "Don't worry, you don't have to go through the bank. Just pay directly to Tom's Autos at 4% over the next five years. What do you say?"

Jeremy was thrilled. After he signed the contract and paid the $1,000, he drove off in his new car with Mike in the passenger seat.

The car gave Jeremy the freedom he had always dreamed of. He took Shannon to parties and to the prom; he did everything in that car, and all he had to do was make a payment to Tom's Autos every three months.

On the second anniversary of the purchase, he learned from one of his friends that Tom's Autos had gone into bankruptcy. Jeremy was worried about the loan he had signed, but as time went by and no one called about it, it became clear no one knew it even existed. Jeremy and his friends realized that the loans they had all signed were not listed as assets in the bankruptcy filing. It was obvious tax evasion on the part of Tom, they all laughed. Jeremy was the owner of a $5,999 car he had paid less than $3,000 for.

When Jeremy turned thirty, he began working for a trucking company. He was on the road for weeks at a time. He travelled long distances throughout Ontario, hauling all kinds of frozen foods, whether they were dairy, orange juice, meat and poultry. He enjoyed the driving as much as he had when he bought his first car at the age of seventeen. That old car was long ago scrapped and a distant memory, as was Shannon, who was now married and living out of province.

During his long hauls, Jeremy was wont, like many other truckers, to pick up hitchhikers. It was frowned upon, but it helped break up the routine. It was during one of these long hauls that he was approached at a truck stop by a woman he assumed to be a prostitute. She could not have been much older than twenty-two. She had long brown hair, was of medium height and weight, and wore tight shorts, a black tee shirt, and boots laced up to her calves. Being unmarried, he thought she would be good company. Once inside the cab of his truck, she turned to Jeremy and asked him a very strange question.

"Are you a religious man?"

"No," he laughed.

"I heard this crazy riddle from some guy. Maybe you can answer it for me."

"Okay, I guess. Shoot."

"Well, imagine, right, like in the movies, the Devil, he offers you a bargain: your soul for something, right?"

"Yeah …"

"Well, imagine that instead he sold you something. How would you pay it back?"

"I don't understand."

"Well, there's no money in hell. You can't take it with you, right? So how would you pay it back."

"I don't follow you."

"Like, if you had to work, how many years do you think you would have to work to pay it back? An eternity, right?"

"I don't get it."

"Well, you make nothing in hell, right? So, to make that money, you've gotta work a pretty long time."

"Look, I don't get it, and any way I'm not religious," he said and turned away to start up his truck.

"It doesn't matter if you're religious or not. For example, let's say you buy a car and you don't pay for it, but as it turns out the whole thing was a setup because now you have to pay me an eternity of work. Right?"

Jeremy turned back towards her. He knew he was definitely stumped.

Seen It All
Heard It All

Having practiced family law for twelve years, Sandra had seen it all; she had heard it all. When her own marriage teetered on the brink of ruin, she knew exactly what needed to be done. She had been married to Thomas for six years and they had been together for a total of eight, and her love for him was as strong as ever. Average in appearance and temperament, his was a happy average, and it complemented her own so very well. He made her laugh; he gave her joy, and now he gave her heartache. Sandra definitely knew what had to be done.

Her own crisis came while she was dealing with a client embroiled in a firestorm of a divorce. Sandra had seen it all, she had heard it all, and here she was doing it all over again. Her client, a tall woman with a strong personality, had been referred to her by a colleague who found her impossible to work with. In her first session, she told Sandra her husband was a consummate philanderer. In their seven years of marriage, the man had almost certainly had more sex outside their marriage than inside it. He cheated on her with everyone. He had cheated with her friends to the point she no longer had any. He cheated with people he knew at work as a bus driver; he cheated with the people who boarded the bus. The man cheated with everyone. The woman was sure there was something wrong with him and demanded Sandra have him tested for the cheating gene. She had heard about it from her mother, who told her that even her own father, who Sandra's client had not seen since she was very young, had it. Her mother explained to her that it acted like a virus and that she had caught him trying to spread it to the neighbours and some of her friends. When Sandra told her there was no such thing, she refused to believe it. She insisted it must exist, and considering how her husband behaved, it would be easy to find since he must have an extra-large chromosome of it.

Sandra believed she had heard it all. But then came the financial settlement stage. With her client, her client's husband, and his lawyer together in the same room, the woman demanded he return her kidney. It turned out, several years earlier, her husband had become deathly ill and gone into renal failure. Needing a new kidney, she proved to be an ideal match, so she donated one of her own. She now wanted it back. She made it very clear that if he didn't return it voluntarily, that it be taken by force. Sandra pulled her aside and tried to explain to her that such a thing would be impossible to do, but the woman didn't care. If they couldn't transplant it back to her, then they should give it to someone else; failing that, just throw it away.

Sandra thought she had seen it all, that she had heard it all until, her own husband, the man who still made her feel alive all these years later, threatened to leave her … unless he got a pet goat. Surprised as she was, she knew what needed to be done. First, she tried to reason with him. She tried to explain to Thomas that having a farm animal live inside a house was generally not done. She then asked him where they would find goat feed in the city, but Thomas just looked away. He was a man who knew what he wanted, and he was adamant about it. He wanted a pet goat, and he would leave her if he had to.

Sandra had seen it all, and she had heard it all, so when all else failed, she knew what needed to be done. She and Thomas adopted a jumping, frolicking little goat irrespective of the fact they lived in Toronto's exclusive Rosedale. When their friends came over (there were fewer and fewer of them over time), they would see the little animal, hopping and bouncing from room to room. It would butt its pretty little head against all the furniture, knocking over antique cabinets and vases with boundless enthusiasm. They watched in amazement as the perfect little animal happily munched on the curtains, the couch, and anything else it was able to fasten those pretty molars onto.

As much as it was a chore cleaning its diaper and a headache finding it feed in the middle of Toronto, Sandra's husband was happy with his perfect goat, and their marriage lasted. That, it turns out, was something their friends (who no longer visited anymore) couldn't say about their own.

Throughout the years that animal bounced and hopped from room to room, Sandra tried everything she could to convince Thomas that next time they should get a dog, a cat, a budgie, or maybe a goldfish. Yes, a goldfish, because what could possibly go wrong with a goldfish? Thomas rarely said anything at such times, and that always left Sandra in fear that he might develop an interest in a cow, a donkey, or God forbid, a rhinoceros or a giraffe.

The Forever Couple

I t's one of those things about getting older: you end up spending more and more of your time thinking about the past and the choices you've made. Every once in a while, now, I catch myself thinking of Chloe and sometimes I even think about the Forever Couple.

Chloe was such a pretty woman. She had short, dark brown hair and a most beautiful name. I had known her since our years at university: she, on her way to becoming a legal assistant, and I, a financial consultant. We laughed at the same jokes, enjoyed the same movies, and listened to the same music. Many of the friends we had back then assumed we would become a couple, but we never did; we just stayed, as always, good friends.

It was from Chloe that I learned of the Forever Couple. I didn't know what she meant by it at first, but she told me about a couple from her place of work .They were the

Taylors, and they worked in the firm's law library, stacking the shelves. The two were two peas in a pod: what he did, she did; what she said, he said. They were a forever force in a constantly changing universe; entanglement was their state of being from beginning to end.

I didn't really spend any time thinking about them because I had just too many things to do. Over the next few weeks, I made my way through western Ontario, providing updates to our clients on various issues related to a software package our company had released, and I didn't see Chloe for a while. When I returned to my apartment in the downtown core of Toronto, the first person who called was, of course, Chloe. It was nice to hear from a friend, and she asked how it all went. When I told her I was done in, she laughed.

"I'm serious. I'm thinking of throwing myself out of the window right now."

"Come on, it can't be all that bad. What if I take you out?"

"Now?"

"Sure. There's someone I want you to meet. I've got a date, and I want you there."

I was puzzled, but she wouldn't tell me who the man might be. Chloe had terrible instincts, and nothing ever worked out for her. I put on a jacket and headed over to T.K.'s, which was our usual haunt. It was there I met for the first time the Forever Couple. I was surprised Chloe would do that to me. I sat across from them, and we began to talk about various things, and it was uncanny. They were exactly as Chloe had said. They were inextricably linked to each other. They spoke, it seemed, a language that was all their own. All their thoughts seemed to be choreographed and rehearsed as if they came from a central place deep within the well of their beings.

After our meal, the Taylors headed out. I was about to leave Chloe to her date when she let me know there wasn't one. With that, I took Chloe to a bar across the street. As we waited for our drinks, Chloe asked, "What did you think?"

"Well, it was … interesting."

Chloe laughed. "Yeah. You know, of all the people I've ever gone out with, I didn't have anything in common with any of them."

I didn't say anything because I knew what she meant. So instead, I said, "What about me?" and we both laughed.

I was home for only a month before I was on the road yet again, this time out to Montreal. I held a number of discussion groups, explaining something I can't talk about even now because it's so confusing, and then I came back to Toronto. The following day I received a call from Chloe. She was excited. I asked what was wrong. She told me the Forever Couple had broken up. I was bewildered at first, then I remembered the couple from T.K.'s. I asked Chloe how it had happened. Chloe told me a young female temporary assistant had been hired, and she and he had hooked up. I was somewhat surprised and really didn't want to know anymore. Chloe then asked if we could get together later, but I had to tell her I would be far too busy. I needed to be back in Montreal in a few days to clear up some issues, and then I needed to head out to Vancouver, but maybe when I got back in a couple of weeks.

"It's alright. Work right now is a killer, but when you get back, call me."

"Sure, Chloe, you'll be the first one I call," I said, and fell on my bed, exhausted.

Travelling was the worst part of my job. It ate up most of my social life, so meeting up with Chloe was something I looked forward to. People I'd known since elementary school and played softball in the park with I didn't see around anymore. Friends from university got married and had kids, and many didn't even live in the city anymore. Marriages have a strange way of creating one family while breaking up another.

When I got back to Toronto, the first person I called was Chloe. She told me she had news. I hoped it wasn't about our couple, but she wouldn't say. She invited me to T.K.'s and that I should come around seven.

Thankfully the traffic wasn't too bad, and I arrived at just past seven. The place was still fairly empty. I saw Chloe sitting with a drink, so I quietly sat down beside her. She turned excitedly and hugged me. I wondered more than ever why we had never become a couple. For the first time I saw her as the beautiful woman she was. She was strong, independent with a fierce temper but a beautiful heart. I looked into her eyes, and she blushed.

"So, what's the news?" I hoped it wasn't that she was engaged.

"They're together again."

"Oh," and I relaxed. It was the couple again.

"They're here."

"Where?" I said, and I began to turn.

Chloe grabbed my arm. "Don't. Be discreet."

I slowly turned, and in the window seat I made out the Taylors. They sat silently, mostly staring down at the table. It seemed as if they were warding off a world that was more dangerous than either had ever known. As I watched them, I again thought about Chloe and myself. Were we destined to be a Forever Couple like the Taylors, or would we continue to move in parallel, never to meet? I turned back and ordered a drink. I then asked Chloe what else was going on in her life.

Sir Pronghorn Academy

It was very early in the school year when our daughter's new school let us know in no uncertain terms that we were doing things very wrong. They had sent us a letter informing us that if we did not correct the situation, we would be forced to take our daughter to another school. My wife and I were surprised and requested a meeting with the school principal. He agreed to meet us only if we agreed to keep our conversation private. We did, but …

When we arrived for our appointment, we were welcomed by the school principal. He was taller than me, and I'm just above average height. Dressed in a blue suit, he had a head shaped like the crock pot my wife cooked rice in. A schoolteacher, not my daughter's, was with him. She was so tiny we had originally mistaken her for one of the students, but she was definitely a school teacher. The woman had an angular face, which must have been of some assistance in explaining geometry. She had long brown hair that she tied in the back. While the principal sat behind a massive desk, she sat in a chair to the side of it.

My wife and I sat in two chairs set in front of the principal's massive desk and waited to find out what we had done so very wrong that it drew the ire of the school. Sir Pronghorn Academy was a highly respected institution. All our friends, and their friends, enrolled their children there. They all seemed well cared for, and all the children did very well academically. When it came time to make a decision as to what school to send our daughter, it was an easy decision to make. Melissa was our only child, and at seven she was a mischievous little girl, full of life and energy.

The man began in the following way: "Yes, Mr. and Mrs. Sciarra, we aspire to the highest standards here at Sir Pronghorn Academy, as you well know. We hold all these dear children in our protecting hands," and he demonstrated how, I suppose, you might throttle a chicken. "If you can't match our commitments to excellence, we sadly must decline your son's further education."

"Son? It's our daughter," I corrected.

"Oh." and he looked down at the documents that were laid out on his desk. "Yes, yes. Your daughter .You see, in the last few days, It's come to our attention that your family has no monsters."

"Monsters?" my wife, an excitable woman, said aloud.

"Yes. Monsters. You see, we have here at Sir Pronghorn Academy a policy that requires all our students have at least one terrifying beast under their bed at night. It makes them, shall we say, more amenable to the teaching experience. You see," (he seemed to like that expression a lot) "here at Sir Pronghorn Academy, our teachers feel that a sensitive child is a teachable child. A child more inclined to attend classes with vigour and learn all the wonderful things we have to offer here at Sir Pronghorn Academy."

We were confused, so my wife said, "But monsters aren't real."

"Oh, it's not important that they be real. What is important is that the children believe they are real. Monsters are necessary!" and he slammed the desk. I thought he was squashing a fly.

I don't understand what we're supposed to do. Get a monster? Where exactly are we supposed to get one?" I laughed nervously, not wishing to offend him.

"Now, I understand," and he looked at my wife and me, who were casually dressed, "some people cannot afford a good, powerfully ugly beast, like some of our more, shall we say, better endowed parents. Some children here at Sir Pronghorn Academy have several monsters. Why, we had two moppets, Jimmy and Cyndi, who had six of them. One each under their beds at night, one each in their closets, and one each scratching the bedroom walls just after bedtime. They were excellent children. Very open to all we have to offer here at Sir Pronghorn Academy. You could maybe take out a loan from a bank?"

"But monsters aren't real," my wife repeated.

"Real, schmeel! Who cares if they're not real!" and he slammed his desk again, "You see" (again with that "you see"), "at Sir Pronghorn Academy we need monsters. Big, filthy, hairy creatures to keep these … children under control. A sensitive child is a teachable child. If you can't supply your child with the requisite monster, I'm sadly going to have to ask you to take your son—"

"Daughter," I corrected.

"Yes, yes, daughter—she will need to go elsewhere."

"But how would you even know if the child actually has a monster?" my wife asked.

"Oh ,we know. We can spot children that have monsters. They have a way about them. You know," and he leaned over, "all our staff had monsters when they were children." He then leaned back. "I myself had a pair of brutes until I was seventeen, and they were devils, real devils. And take a look at me now, all these years later. Why, I'm principal at this very academy," he smiled broadly.

"But how exactly would you be able to tell?" my wife asked again.

"Children with monsters," the teacher piped in, "are sensitive children. They're always looking around."

"Very reassuring, you know, to see a child playing and then … bang! A loud noise, and they scurry like little rats. Very … reassuring," the principal added with a smile.

My wife and I were more confused than ever.

"So, anyway, your son—"

"Daughter," I corrected.

"Yes, yes—your daughter will have one week to shape up or … unfortunately she will need to go to another school. Maybe the one up the road," and he laughed. "Thank you for your time. And remember: one week," and he reached out his hand.

My wife and I didn't know what to think. As I mentioned before, the school had come highly recommended; all of our friends sent their children to it. I wondered if we should consider a different school, but then my wife reminded me we wouldn't be able to do that unless we moved. We were trapped.

Melissa was such a happy child. She was curious, free spirited—all the things you hope your child would be.

That night, we asked her about her friends, we played a few games after dinner, and then we sent her up to brush her teeth. It took a bit of effort, but finally, with a kiss from her mom and me, she was tucked into bed. We then closed the lights and the door and retreated to the room next to hers. The room was at one time going to be a bedroom for a second child, but Melissa was beautiful enough, and we now used it as our office. My wife went up to the wall and began to scratch, while I thumped on the wall in imitation of a beating heart. As we continued in this way, I began to wonder if maybe a scary toy would be a good idea too.

Alessandro's Last Stand

The world changed for Alessandro when he visited his son's twenty-three year old girlfriend, Cora. Alessandro had been looking forward to surprising her with a basket of the tomatoes that she so desired that he had not bothered to phone first. When he drove into the parking garage of the apartment building where his son, Emilio and Cora lived, he was confused as to whose vehicle was now parked in their reserved parking spot. Alessandro decided to circle to the front of the building and park there. He then walked up to the building, and luckily for him, the lobby door swung open. Two laughing young girls came out .

Alessandro walked across the lobby floor, got on the elevator, and started up to the sixth floor. Being a family man, he and his wife Beatrice were so very pleased when Emilio introduced them to Cora. Finally, finally, they thought, he's going to settle down. At twenty-nine their son was almost eight years older than Alessandro and Beatrice had been when they had wed. What made Beatrice especially happy was knowing that slim, raven haired, and pretty Cora was from an Italian family that hailed from a town in Italy her own parents came from. Now that the two had been together for just over a year, she could not stop asking when they would be getting married.

Alessandro got off the elevator with his basket and walked to their apartment, which was at the end of the hall next to the stairwell. As he approached, Alessandro could hear the laughter of Cora and someone else. When he knocked on the door, the laughter abruptly stopped. After what seemed like an eternity, Alessandro tapped on the door yet again. It was at least a minute before the door opened a crack, and he saw the angelic face of Cora peep out. Cora smiled, and in a trembling voice Alessandro told her he had brought the tomatoes from his garden that she so liked. She thanked him and told him to put them down by the door and that she would pick them up later. Alessandro did as he was told and left. As he pressed the elevator button, he was sure he heard laughter coming from down the hall.

Alessandro went down the elevator and out to his car. He was upset and tried to understand what had just happened. He knew that Emilio worked late, so whose car was parked in his spot? Alessandro needed to know. He drove back into the garage and parked several spots down. After almost thirty minutes of waiting, he heard the distinct sound of whistling. A short, balding man carrying a basket of tomatoes walked over to the car. The man placed the basket on the hood of the car and opened the door. Placing the basket in the back seat, he got in and drove out.

Alessandro was confused. He sat and sat and would have sat longer if not for the persistent honk of a car that was soon followed by the loud shouts of a woman demanding he get out of her parking spot. Alessandro drove away. When he got home, he could see Beatrice preparing tomato sauce. The smell of pork and lamb bubbling in tomato sauce was too much of a distraction, so Alessandro went outside to his vegetable garden. He sat at a stone table he had built several years before and looked out at his tomato plants. He knew he couldn't tell his wife or his son until he was certain of what he suspected. After all, he didn't want to alienate Emilio and Cora over what was almost certainly a simple misunderstanding on his part. He would need to check up on his son before doing anything. When Beatrice began cooking spaghetti, Alessandro went about his garden, tying vines that needed tying, pulling out plants that needed pulling out, and of course, he did a lot of thinking.

The following day, Alessandro made his way to the landscaping business that his son largely ran on his own. Alessandro had established it a quarter of a century before, and through hard work, had made it into a success. When his son finished high school and then received a certificate in finance from college, he joined the company full-time. Emilio had already been helping out since he was a young teenager, so it was a seamless fit. Over the course of the previous year, Alessandro had been leaving more and more of its daily operations to his son, so that he now only came in whenever landscaping work needed to be done. At such times he could be seen moving slabs of stone and gravel with a front loader.

When Alessandro entered, he could see his son dealing with customers. He watched as his son laughed at some joke and then later, offered suggestions to a couple. Nothing seemed out of order. When his son came over, Alessandro watched him closely. They talked for a while, and it soon became clear to Alessandro that he must be mistaken about Cora. Leaving, he decided that he needed to pay her a visit and see how she was doing, since they had not spoken the day before.

Cora was such a beautiful girl. Ever since his son had introduced her, he had considered her to be the daughter he and Beatrice had never had. Alessandro enjoyed spending time talking to her, laughing with his son and the woman who had stolen his heart. When his wife and her sister teased him that he had a thing for the girl, he would tell them to quit it. He didn't find it at all funny.

Alessandro drove the few miles that it took to his son and girlfriend's apartment and entered the parking garage where, yet again, he was taken by surprise. In Emilio's parking spot was yet another unfamiliar car. Alessandro parked a little further down than last time and stewed. He knew he had to get to the bottom of this sordid mess, and so he waited. Eventually, a tall, thin man, walked over, got into the car, and drove off. Alessandro didn't know exactly what he ought to do. He sat and tried to calm down. He knew he had to speak to Cora, but first he would need to move his car into his son's parking spot, or who knows what might happen.

His mind a mess, Alessandro made his way up the elevator to the sixth floor. As he approached, he could distinctly hear the sound of running water coming from the apartment. Alessandro knocked on the door. It opened a crack, and the smiling, angelic Cora peeped out. Seeing it was Alessandro, she opened the door and let him in. She had obviously just finished bathing because her hair was wet and she was wrapped in a robe.

Alessandro crossed to the couch. It was not a large apartment; the living room also doubled as a dining room. The television set was across from the couch against the wall, and the dining table was pushed to the far end by the patio doors that led out to the balcony. Without a word, Alessandro sat down. Cora smiled. Alessandro could not understand why. He continued to sit quietly, and she continued smiling. He couldn't stand that smile any longer, so he rose and, arms outstretched, he shouted, "Do you like this?"

Cora smiled and bobbed her head up and down. That was a bit of a surprise, considering Alessandro was beginning to resemble the front loader he used for landscaping.

He was more confused than ever. Not knowing what to say that would stop her smiling, he pulled his pants down and again shouted, "Do you like this?"

Cora again smiled and bobbed her head up and down.

With nowhere else to go, Alessandro pulled down his underwear and again shouted, "Do you like this?"

Cora again smiled and bobbed her head up and down.

Not knowing what else he could do that would stop her smiling, he, with great difficulty, pulled Cora to the kitchen table, pushed the chair away, pulled her robe off, and leaned her over.

As Alessandro was thrusting into her, he again shouted, "Do you like this?" From his vantage point he could just make out her smile and the side of her head bobbing up and down.

After Alessandro ejaculated, he released her and pulled up his underwear and pants. As he was doing so, he could see that she was watching him with that same smile. Storming out, he made his way to the elevator and down to his car. In total confusion, he drove back to his house, where Beatrice was watching the soaps. Not saying a word, he went into his garden and sat down. He could not for the life of him fathom what was going on. None of it made any sense. Cora was such a beautiful girl. What was he to do? He thought and thought for what must have been an hour, and yet the only thing he knew for certain at the end of it was that he couldn't tell his wife or son anything until he was completely sure of what exactly was going on. Alessandro knew that he had to go back the next day.

After a good lunch of bread and sausages, Alessandro told his wife he would be going over to the supply store to make sure everything was alright, and he left. On the drive to the apartment, he wondered what he could say to poor Cora. She must have been frightened by all that had happened. As he entered the garage, he was surprised when he saw yet another car parked in Emilio's spot. This was definitely getting out of hand. Like before, Alessandro drove into a free space and waited. This time it wasn't long before a bearded giant of a man walked over, got in, and drove off. Alessandro could not believe what was happening. He sat there and stewed. It must have been ten minutes of torture before he drove his car into his son's spot.

Alessandro quickly made his way up to the sixth floor. Heading down the hall, he could hear the flow of water. As he banged on the door, the strangest thought passed through his mind: these apartments were really cheaply built considering you could hear the shower out in the hallway. When Cora finally opened the door, he could see she was wrapped in the same robe from the previous day. He stormed past her, and as she closed the door, he screamed, "This is what you like to do! This is what you like to do!" To which Cora smiled and bobbed her head up and down.

Alessandro did not know how to frighten her back to her senses, but being the man of action he was, he tore off her robe, hoping that might work. Cora simply looked at him, and laughed. Alessandro did not know how to make her understand, so he did the only thing that passed through his mind: he pulled her to the kitchen table and pulled down his pants and underwear. As Cora looked back at Alessandro, he leaned her over, and with nothing else left to do, he mounted her. As he thrust into her again and again, he shouted, "This is what you like to do! This is what you like to do!"

When Alessandro ejaculated, he could still make out the side of Cora's head bobbing up and down, and oh yes, that smile. Pulling up his underwear and pants, he stormed out in a fury. Getting in his car, Alessandro was so confused he couldn't remember where he lived. It was almost a minute before it came to him, and he was able to drive home.

When he got home, it was clear Beatrice had gone shopping. This would give him time to think. He sat outside for a while. Alessandro then got up and dug holes that didn't need digging, cleared plants that didn't need clearing, and watered grass that didn't need watering. How was he supposed to tell his wife what their son's girlfriend was up to? The whole thing was so sordid it would surely break her heart. Alessandro needed to get through to that girl somehow. He knew he had to go back.

The following day, Alessandro explained to his wife he had a few bills to pay and some customers to see and headed off. As he drove, he tried to come up with some strategy, some way to bring her back to her senses. Alessandro was still deep in thought as he pulled into the garage, and yes, lo and behold, someone else had taken Emilio's parking spot. He waited in complete confusion until a man older than himself walked over to the car. Now he knew he had seen it all. Up to the sixth floor he went. Down the hall he went. Alessandro banged on Cora's door. As he waited, his mind was a whirlwind; he was no longer able to think clearly. What was going on?

Finally, the door opened, and there before him stood the beautiful, naked body of Cora. Alessandro's mind gave way. Cora laughed when he reached out for her because she knew he was lost and would never find himself again.

He Was
Like This ...

There was a man who had been with many women. He had been with so many that it no longer surprised him when some of them talked about their boyfriends, husbands, ex-boyfriends, or ex-husbands. It no longer surprised him when they spoke of how they were like this and how they were like that, how they had done this and how they had done that. He knew by this time they were only getting in the mood.

So it didn't surprise this man, when the woman spoke of her ex-husband. How he was like this and how he was like that; how he had done this and how he had done that, because she only wanted someone to listen to her. So he kissed her on the forehead; he kissed her on the cheek; he kissed her on the eyes as she spoke of her ex-husband, and how he was like this and how he was like that, how he had done this and how he had done that. And so he kissed her as she spoke of her ex-husband, and how he had done this and how he had done that, and he kissed her.

He put his hand on her knee as she spoke of her ex-husband. So he kissed her. He kissed her on the forehead; he kissed her on the cheek as she spoke of her ex-husband, and he kissed her on the mouth. When she kissed him back, he moved his hand up her legs and between them. He watched her as she spoke of her ex-husband, of how he was like this and how he was like that.

He put his fingers inside her as she spoke of her ex-husband, and how he was like this and how he was like that, how he had done this and how he had done that. And he watched her as the words began to circle around and around and around. And he watched her. He watched her when she stopped talking about her ex-husband, about how he was like this and how he was like that, how he had done this and how he had done that. He watched her when her head fell back, and he stroked her again and again, and he watched her.

And when he was inside her, he thought about her ex-husband and how he was like this and how he was like that, how he had done this and how he had done that.

He thought about her ex-husband and how he was like this and how he was like that, how he had done this and how he had done that.

He thought about her ex-husband …

"I Was Just Stopping By ..."

Jessie had broken up with her boyfriend, Mark, so very many times, and each time they always got back together. She knew he was jealous and possessive, but in a curious way, it gave her a sense of power and importance, and she used it so well. It was also true that Mark's jealousy wasn't always misplaced. Jessie flirted shamelessly, and several times she took it far beyond just innocent flirting. It was an exciting thing to be young and desirable, and Jessie was definitely that. Tall and thin with long black hair, Jessie had eyes that never looked away.

Tonight she would be meeting Mark, so she wanted a drink to calm her nerves. They had not seen each other in a month, and he had called her and apologized for all his misplaced anger. She sat at the bar and ordered herself a drink. Tony poured the dark liquid into a glass and smiled. She had never had sex with Tony, but they knew each other so very well. Tony, after all, had been the best man at her brother's wedding. He was a few years older than her and overweight, which she found to be a turnoff. Jessie sipped on her drink and thought of what she would say to Mark when—

"Why, I can't believe it. It is you, isn't it?"

Startled, she turned her head. The man was short and balding and very thin; although she couldn't tell his age, he was definitely older than her.

"Mmm?" she said, swallowing her drink.

"It is you. I was walking by and came in without thinking, and there you were. I've been looking for you for quite a while. There's so much to talk about."

"Do I know you?" she asked.

"Why, I hope so. It's just that we always seem to be going in opposite directions."

"I don't understand. What do you mean?"

"I've been looking for you for quite a while, quite a while. And now here you are," he laughed.

"I still don't understand what you're saying. I think you have the wrong person."

"Oh no. I have the right person. It is you, and here we are finally."

"I think you're wrong. I think you'd better leave me alone," and she turned away.

"Leave you alone? Leave you alone? But I can't do that now."

"Tony!" Jessie called out, but Tony had gone to the back to check the inventory.

"Tony, Tony, Tony," he said. "It's Mark you should be—"

Jessie cut him off. "How do you know Mark?"

"I know a lot of things, Jessie. I know a lot of things."

"How do you know my name? Who are you? What is this? Did Mark send you here?"

"Mark? Oh no, Mark doesn't know I'm here."

"You know Mark? How do you know Mark?" she asked.

"I don't know Mark, exactly, no, no— but I do know you, and when I came in there you were," and he laughed again.

"Who are you? Is this a gag? Who sent you here?"

"No one sent me here, Jessie. Seriously. I was just walking by and happened to come in, and there you were."

"Look, you're creeping me out. I'm going," and Jessie picked up her handbag and made to leave.

"Sure. Go Jessie. After all, you don't want to keep him waiting," he said in a quiet, menacing tone.

"What does that mean!" she said, turning to face him.

"Well, you know better than me. After all, Mark is jealous and possessive. Oh yes. He is very, very possessive."

"How do you know Mark? Who are you?" she screamed.

"You keep asking such useless questions, you know," he said, looking away.

"Look, if you don't tell me what this is all about, I'm going to call the cops," she threatened.

"You could do that. You could do that, I suppose. But like I said, I just stopped in, and you were here. There's no harm in that, is there?"

"Look, I'm going," and she turned to leave.

"You better, Jessie. He can be incredibly violent," he said in a low tone.

"How do you know Mark?" she screamed. " Where is Tony?" But he was still in the stockroom sorting out the inventory.

"Tony, Tony, Tony," he repeated.

"Where is everyone?" she screamed, looking around her at the empty bar.

"Oh, please, it's a slow day, is all. Don't worry, people come in all the time. There will be people enough, Jessie."

"Stop using my name! You don't know me!" she screamed.

"But it is your name, Jessie, isn't it?"

She was confused and began walking toward the door.

"Tell Mark I'll be catching up with him soon, and we'll have ourselves a long talk," he said menacingly.

As Jessie was stepping outside the door, she could hear him talking to Tony.

"Can you believe it? I was walking by, minding my own business, when I decided to step in for a drink. Of all the people I could run into, I run into Jessie. It's a strange world, you know," and he began to laugh.

Rachel

When I was younger, I worked for a bank. In my third year, I was assigned to manage one of the bank's branches. The branch was located in a small town I had never heard of. It was a small place that lay far from the outskirts of any larger town. This town had only two general stores. While they both offered similar items, it was the Centre Street General that was the true heart of the community. It was owned and operated by a married couple, and unlike its counterpart, this store also served as a post office and as a general-purpose pharmacy. It was the community hub: the spokes of that little town emanated from it.

I, as everyone who knows me can attest, am not a religious man. While I do believe in a force that drives all that is possible, I don't feel it's ever been written in any religious text. The owners of that shop, on the other hand, were very religious; he far more than she. Her name was Rachel, and his was James. Rachel was a very attractive woman with deep, soulful brown eyes. Clichéd, maybe, but the brown of those eyes matched the color of her hair. She often heightened the overall effect with the color of her dresses.

Rachel had married when she was only a few years past her teens to the older James. While she came from a close family that still called the town home, I rarely heard James speak of his. Although the two had planned on having children, it became clear early on that Rachel was unable to bear children, and so they moved on.

Now, while Rachel had a warm and generous personality, James was an intense individual. With hair that had begun greying prematurely, he was thinner than his wife but as tall, with eyes that seemed to look straight through you. Cliché? As we get older, we all strive to live a cliched life. While James taught Sunday School to the town's children on weekends, the rest of the week he lectured to anyone who would listen his opinions on the evils of modern living. While this might have been an issue elsewhere, it wasn't here because, as I said, it was a small town with two general stores. Whenever there was a lull in business, which was quite often, he could be found railing against the evils of the flesh. They needed to be controlled, vanquished, for there could be no respite until then. If I happened to be in the Centre General at such times, I couldn't stop myself looking across at poor Rachel, her eyes burning, burning, burning, and fear for her beautiful soul.

Now, as rigid and narrow as James was, he did have one weakness, and it was with alcohol: he could not handle it at all. He almost never drank, but when he did, it was generally only a glass or two on special occasions. At such times, he would quickly become drunk and would have to be put to bed, or the man would shed his soul like the skin of a snake. I've often wondered if Rachel discouraged or encouraged her husband at such times. Other than that, the two lived a quiet existence in a big house on the edge of this very small town.

It was during my second year as manager of the local bank that I became aware that Rachel's younger sister, Annie, was to be married. It was a joyous announcement; Rachel, it turned out, even knew the boy as one she and a girlfriend had teased mercilessly in elementary school. Rachel congratulated her little sister and offered her help in preparing for the special day. Annie happily accepted, and the two, with the help of their mother and several close girlfriends, spent the next four months working tirelessly on all the details. The dress was going to be the one Rachel had worn to her own wedding and her mother had worn to hers; the church would be the one they prayed in every Sunday. The banquet hall proved to be a difficult thing to arrange in such a small town, which meant sacrificing many potential guests. Only family and the closest of friends were invited to the momentous occasion. The only reason I was invited was probably the two mortgages my bank held on their house and business. In any event, the four months flew by so quickly that it must have left Rachel with a nagging feeling something would surely go wrong to spoil the whole celebration.

The wedding turned out to be a beautiful occasion. Annie was resplendent in her wedding gown, and the groom was a handsome specimen in his tuxedo. Vows were read. The groom then kissed the bride, and the congregation, as they always do, wept. It was the beginning of the most blessed of unions. With congratulations all around, the rest of the celebration began.

Rachel, the always beautiful Rachel, was definitely in high spirits. Her father and mother positively beamed. The newlyweds danced, they held each other, and when they kissed, the room erupted. James, I could see, drank his first glass.

When the father of the groom, a big man with a barrel for a chest, tried to sing, his wife, quite a bit smaller, laughed and slapped at him to sit down. The groom rose to give a toast. His closest friends laughed with him as he spoke of his happiness and the promise that awaited. His friends then gave their own toasts, complimenting the beautiful Annie and the wonderful family she came from. Annie cried, and of course so did Rachel. James, I could see, drank another glass. Rachel, I guess, must have thought it was all right. It would do him good to have some fun.

They all danced and laughed, and cried about life and how important it is to have someone there who you care about and who cares about you. It is that, after all, which makes all the tragedies we endure bearable. The food was wonderful, I wish I could say, but anyway … With the night joyous, James drank some more. Let's face it, at this point, James was drunk. The man, always on the alert against the sins of the flesh, attempted a dance with the beautiful Rachel that should have been kept to their bedroom. Rachel laughed and pushed James's hands away; the crowd, of course, cheered him on.

When the final toast was given, and the guests told to drive carefully, the bride and groom were long gone, as was I. The following details I've been told by a very good authority. Rachel and James were far too drunk to drive home by themselves, as was Rachel's father; with Rachel's mother unwilling to be in a car with James, the groom's father was conscripted.

This man had been agreeable during the celebrations, but I knew a different side to him through his dealings at my bank. The man was as tightfisted as they come and more prickly than a porcupine. He was a constant head-ache, always demanding better and better terms on every-thing. For example, the car that James was poured into had only recently been bought by way of a ridiculously generous loan from my bank. When Rachel got into the back seat, she better have apologized for the inconvenience.

Now, I have to admit this car trip didn't actually happen this way, but it's too fitting not to have. (Yes, I really despise the man.) The barrel on two legs didn't say a word but instead kept his eyes firmly fixed on James. As he slowly drove, Rachel could see him watching them from his interior rearview mirror. Now, slowly is not always slow enough, and that proved to be the case here; James, being too drunk to know any better, and the car newly purchased by way of a ridiculously generous loan from my bank, vomited on the car's new upholstery. Rachel did her best to clean the night's dinner from the upholstery in that car, which that barrel on two legs had bought using my bank's money, but all she ended up accomplishing was to grind it in more. Now we can get back to our story. When they finally arrived at their house, the man and Rachel pulled James out, and of course, Rachel apologized yet again for all the inconveniences they had put him through. With a grudging goodbye, the barrel drove off in my bank's money.

Now that they were home, Rachel directed James up the steps to their front door. As she began fumbling for the keys, James started fumbling under her dress. She squealed when James appeared to find what he was looking for. With an extra effort, she managed to get the door open, and down they both fell. He was on top of her and must have been more than willing to let it stay that way, but Rachel had work to do. She pushed him off, and James slowly rose to his feet. It must have been a little strange, maybe even thrilling, for Rachel to see a laughing James, but she still needed to get him up the stairs. Closing the door with James's arm around her shoulder would be the easy part, but heaving him up those stairs ... now that would take real effort. With Rachel leaning against him to keep him from tumbling back, and him grabbing whatever beautiful part of Rachel that was available, they made their way up. When the bedroom came into view, James very naturally became energized, so that it was easy to maneuver the man onto their bed. Rachel pulled off his shoes and pants, and only then did she remove her own shoes and dress. She did it all without even turning on the lights.

Lying down beside James, she was sure her ordeal was at an end. Not quite. In the dark it's not always clear, and sometimes one hole is as good as the other, and his wife, being of sound mind and body, was taken aback, so to speak. As God is in heaven and the Devil is in hell, she screamed. Alcohol or not, the poor man was shaken to his core.

James leaped from his bed and would have thrown himself from the second-floor window if it had not been shut tight. The man then fell to his knees in a panic. His clouded brain must have tried to count how many sins he had just committed. That mind, normally narrow but very clear, must have twisted through a great many convolutions that night. And Rachel? Well, she simply lay on the bed with the covers pulled up to her pretty chin, watching the writhing wretch on the floor.

Now, we had been told time and time again by James that unwholesome sex was the gateway sin to the soul, and yet here he found himself in a terrible bind. Whether what had happened was a sin or not, mattered little to him. What did matter was how he could confess such a thing. Even he had his limits. He attempted numerous times and was never up to the task. How many Hail Marys? How many of Our Fathers? He didn't know. Sin or not, he couldn't reconcile himself to what had happened. He spent days and nights in turmoil. Consumed by the guilt, I was told, he bathed three times a day and claimed that flames were hurtling from below. Unable to come to terms with what had happened, James looked more and more inward, which of course, left Rachel to look more and more outward. And I? Well, I managed a bank in a small town far from the outskirts of any larger town.

That, which you've just read, is a story I gave my literary agent. He read it, sat back, and then he told me my life wasn't good enough for fiction. It wasn't the barrel he had a problem with; it was the religious theme he didn't care for. Seen that, done that, he told me.

"What about the beautiful Rachel?" I asked.

"Rachel?" he said to me. "She just doesn't have that punch that comes from a good shot of whisky." (Don't ask me because I don't know what that means.)

"So, what's missing?" I asked.

Sitting back, he stared off into space for a while, and then he said, " Serial killers. Every good story has at least one, but your story doesn't have any. Just make James a serial killer, and turn Rachel into a police detective who goes about chasing him down. Now that's a story that can sell!"

I couldn't believe what I was hearing. When I explained to him I wasn't going to turn my life into that, he informed me his firm would no longer be representing me, and that I would need to find myself another agent. And so, that's that.

www.ingramcontent.com/pod-product-compliance
Lightning Source LLC
Chambersburg PA
CBHW031402060726
47590CB00007B/2900